PASSOVER, HERE I COME!

In memory of Baba Florence and Zeida Max—DJS

To my zeyde Erich Anton Kunz, whom I never met—EW

GROSSET & DUNLAP
An imprint of Penguin Random House LLC, New York

First published in the United States of America by Grosset & Dunlap,
an imprint of Penguin Random House LLC, New York, 2022

Text copyright © 2022 by David Steinberg
Illustrations copyright © 2022 by Emanuel Wiemans

GROSSET & DUNLAP is a registered trademark of Penguin Random House LLC.

Visit us online at penguinrandomhouse.com.

Library of Congress Cataloging-in-Publication Data is available.

Printed in the United States of America

ISBN 9780593224038   10 9 8 7 6 5 4 3 2 1 COMM

PASSOVER, HERE I COME!

BY D. J. STEINBERG

ILLUSTRATED BY EMANUEL WIEMANS

GROSSET & DUNLAP

SCRUB-A-DUB-DUB!

Scrub-a-dub-dub! Vroom-zoom-zoom!
Clean up each and every room!
Sweep the dirt and dust away
to welcome in the holiday!

BYE-BYE, BREAD!

Goodbye, Bagel.
Goodbye, Rye.
Sorry, Sourdough, bye-bye.
Nice to know you, Buttered Toast.
(I think I'll miss you the most.)
Passover is almost here,
so you must all disappear.
It's been fun, but bye-bye, Bread—
we're eating Matzoh now instead!

HELLO, MATZOH!

Hello, Matzoh, crunchy treat!
For eight whole days you're what we eat
in matzoh balls
or from the box,
with butter, jam,
with cheese and lox.
On Passover, we all eat lotsa
this flat bread that we call Matzoh!

MADE BY ME!

Take a look over here—see this Seder plate?
I can't wait for our guests to come celebrate.
When they see how pretty our plate's decorated,
I'll tell them that ME, yours truly, made it!

WHAT SYMBOLS ARE ON THE SEDER PLATE?

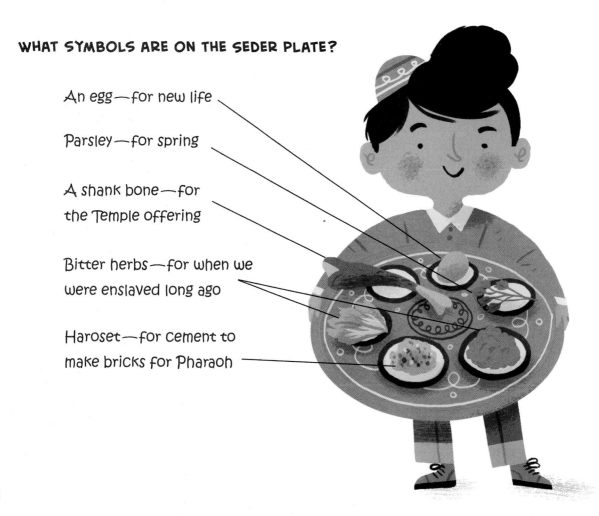

An egg—for new life

Parsley—for spring

A shank bone—for the Temple offering

Bitter herbs—for when we were enslaved long ago

Haroset—for cement to make bricks for Pharaoh

GOTTA GET A HAGGADAH!

Have you got yourself a Haggadah?
It's Passover—you oughta!
You'll need it for the Seder.
Didn't get one yet? You gotta!

OUR MAGIC TABLE

Our table's usually smallish,
but on Passover—what a strange sight!
Somehow our table g r o w s a n d g r o w s
to fit all our Seder guests tonight!

MY WACKY FAMILY

My bubbe gives me a pinch on the cheek.
My zayde pulls coins from my ear.
Aunt Jo slaps her knee and laughs with a shriek
at the jokes Uncle Hersch tells each year.

My cousins all giggle and run from my dad.
If they're caught, upsy-daisy they'll go.
It's the wackiest family in the whole world,
and the very best one that I know!

THE PASSOVER STORY

The Haggadah tells a story
from a long, long time ago
when the Hebrews were enslaved
by the evil King Pharaoh.

A Hebrew hero, Moses,
told him, "Let my people go!"
But guess what mean old Pharaoh answered:
"No, no, no!"
And so . . .

Ten plagues rained down on Egypt
till Pharaoh cried, "Okay!"
and that is when the Hebrew slaves
packed up and ran away.
Moses raised his rod up high—
God parted the Red Sea.
Those Hebrews marched across it
until everyone was free.

And to this day we're thankful
to all be gathered here,
sitting at our Seder
to tell this story every year!

THE FOUR QUESTIONS

Why is this night so different?
Well, one thing I'll tell you . . .
On no other night do I sing the Four Questions,
but on *this* night I do!

MA NISHTANA

"Why is this night different from all the other nights?"

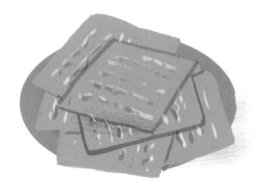

1. Why matzoh, no bread?

2. Why bitter herbs instead?

3. Why foods that we dip?

4. Why recline and not sit?

GRAPE JUICE x4

We drink four cups of grape juice tonight,
we've already finished our first.
Just one-two-three more cups to go . . .
I hope that we don't burst!

DRUM ROLL, PLEASE . . .

Our tummies can't wait one second more—
could it actually be for real?
Brisket is coming through the door—

it's time for the Seder meal!

AND NOW WE INTERRUPT THIS BOOK FOR A VERY IMPORTANT SURVEY

What's the greatest soup in the world?

☐ CHICKEN MATZOH BALL
☐ ONE OF THE OTHERS

(If you didn't check Box 1,
that means you have not tried my mother's!)

GEFILTE FISH

There's no fish in any ocean
that looks anything like that!
It's grayish and it's slimy,
with a little carrot hat.
And there's no way to explain
why grown-ups think that it's delish.
Me, I'd rather eat my shoelace
than go near gefilte fish!

THE SEARCH IS ON!

It's afikomen time,
but our special matzoh's gone!
Grandpa says to find it
or the Seder can't go on!

"Where is it?!" we all shout.
Grandpa shrugs and sighs—
"If one of you can find it,
I'm offering a prize!"

Quick—feel all the pillows.
Check the chairs out to be certain!
By the couch? Beneath the lamp?
Here it is! Behind the curtain!
"We found the afikomen!"
Grandpa shouts out, "Job well done!

Since you did it all together,
here's a prize for EVERYONE!"

WORLD'S BEST BREAKFAST

I can't wait for breakfast.
You want to know why?
Just come to our kitchen—
try some hot matzoh brei!

MOM'S MATZOH BREI

- Mix 4 eggs in a bowl
- Make 2 matzohs wet
- Crumble them in
- Get your fry pan all set
- Fry the mixture in butter
- Add sugar, so sweet
- Sprinkle in salt and pepper
- 2 minutes, serve and EAT!

YOU SHOULD ONLY MAKE THIS RECIPE WITH THE HELP OF A GROWN-UP.

PASSOVER'S OVER

When Passover's over,
first thing on our list
is to run out and get
all the things that we've missed!
Bagels and waffles and pancakes and pie
and three dozen doughnuts . . .
So long, Matzoh—*bye-bye!*